Paddington

MICHAEL BOND

and the
Marmalade Maze

Illustrated by R.W. Alley

Collins

An Imprint of HarperCollins*Publishers*

As they made their way through an arch, Mr Gruber pointed to a large clock.

"That's a very special clock," he said. "It not only shows the time, it tells you what month it is."

"Perhaps we should hurry, Mr Gruber," said Paddington anxiously. "It's half past June already."

Paddington always enjoyed his outings
with Mr Gruber and he couldn't wait to
see inside the Palace.

One day, Paddington's friend, Mr Gruber, took him on an outing to a place called Hampton Court Palace.

"I think you will enjoy it, Mr Brown," he said as they drew near. "It's very old and it has over one thousand rooms. Lots of Kings and Queens have lived here."

"Bears are good at mazes," said Paddington. "You need to be in Darkest Peru. The forests are very thick."

And sure enough, before Mr Gruber had time to say any more, Paddington led the way out, leaving everyone else inside.

"How ever did you manage to do that,
Mr Brown?" gasped Mr Gruber.

"Quickest visit I've ever seen," agreed
the man in the ticket office.

"I used marmalade chunks to show
where we had been," said Paddington. "It's
something my Aunt Lucy taught me before
she went into the Home For Retired Bears."

"But I thought you had eaten all your sandwiches," said Mr Gruber.

"I always keep a spare one under my hat in case I have an emergency," said Paddington. "That's something else Aunt Lucy taught me. She'll be very pleased when she hears."

And he stopped at a kiosk to buy a picture postcard so that he could write and tell her all about his day out.

That night when he went to bed, as well as
the postcard and a pen, Paddington took
some rope.

"It's something Queen Anne used to do,"
he announced. "I've a lot to tell Aunt Lucy
and I don't want to fall out of bed before
I've finished."